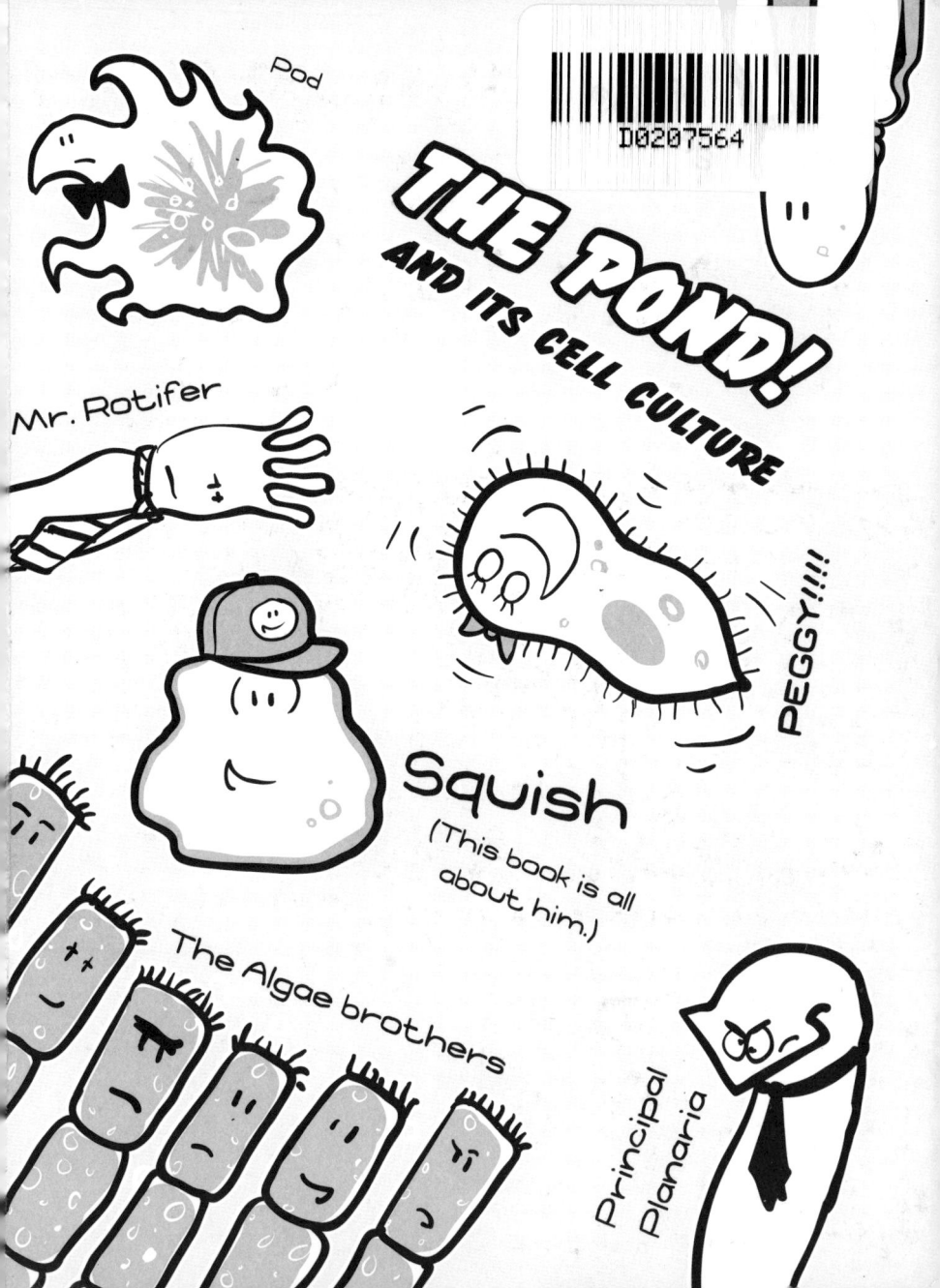

Read ALL the SQUISH books!

#1   SQUISH: Super Amoeba

#2   SQUISH: Brave New Pond

squish
BRAVE NEW POND

BY JENNIFER L. HOLM & MATTHEW HOLM

RANDOM HOUSE NEW YORK

Copyright © 2011 by Jennifer Holm and Matthew Holm
All rights reserved. Published in the United States by
Random House Children's Books,
a division of Random House, Inc., New York.
Random House and the colophon are
registered trademarks of Random House, Inc.

Visit us on the Web! www.randomhouse.com/kids
Educators and librarians, for a variety of teaching tools,
visit us at www.randomhouse.com/teachers

Library of Congress Cataloging-in-Publication Data
Holm, Jennifer L.
Brave new pond / by Jennifer L. Holm and
Matthew Holm. – 1st ed.   p. cm.
Summary: Starting a new school year, Squish, a meek amoeba
who loves the comic book exploits of his favorite hero,
"Super Amoeba," is determined to get picked for kickball
and hang out with the cool kids.
ISBN 978-0-375-84390-7 (trade) –
ISBN 978-0-375-93784-2 (lib. bdg.)
1. Graphic novels. [1. Graphic novels. 2. Amoeba–Fiction.
3. Popularity–Fiction. 4. Superheroes–Fiction.
5. Schools–Fiction.] 1. Holm, Matthew. II. Title.
PZ7.7.H65Br 2011   741.5'973–dc22   2010028084

MANUFACTURED IN MALAYSIA 10 9 8 7 6 5 4 3 2
First Edition

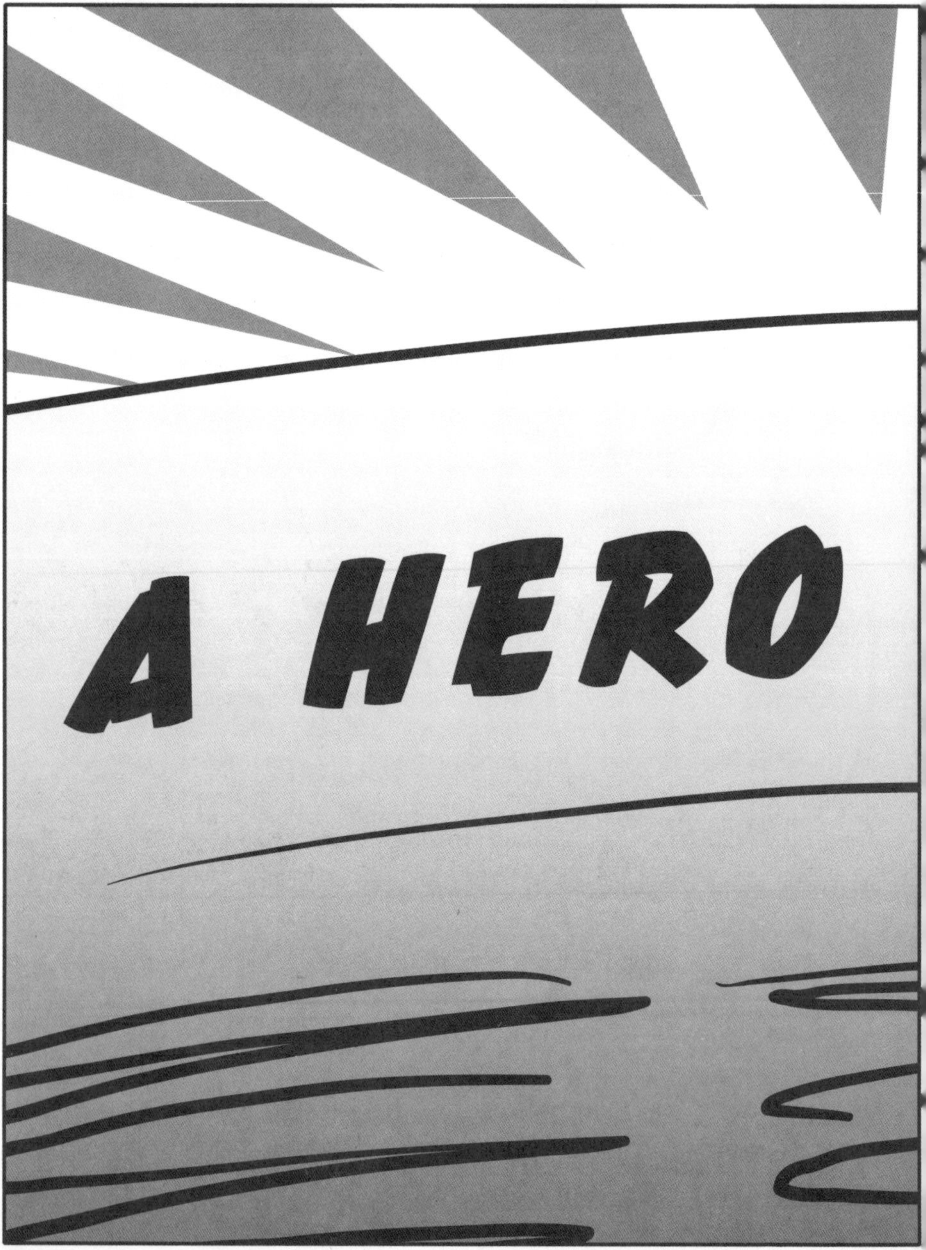
A HERO

8

KEY TO SMALL POND

HELP!

WHIP!

WHEN TROUBLE CALLS . . .

9

SUPER AMOEBA ANSWERS!

ZWOOSH!

ZOOOOOOOOM!

AAH!

SWOOP!

UH, WHAT SEEMS TO BE THE PROBLEM?

MY ICE CREAM FELL! WAAAAHH!

SIGH.

ONE CHOCOLATE, PLEASE.

ICE CREAM

SNIFF! THANKS, SUPER AMOEBA!

WOBBLE

SPLAT!

PLOP!

ICE CR

WAAAAHH!

SIGH.

Do you need lunch money, Squish?

Sigh.

13

 NO TRADING FOOD WITH POD!

 NO DETENTION!

 DO NOT LET PEGGY EMBARRASS ME!

 GET PICKED FOR KICKBALL AT RECESS!

 SIT WITH COOL KIDS AT LUNCH!

 BE COOL!

20

24

Pod?

here. at least until the asteroid hits and we all die.

ROLL

The Algae brothers?

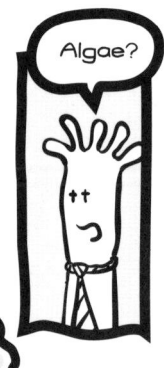

Algae?

Brothers?

SLAM!

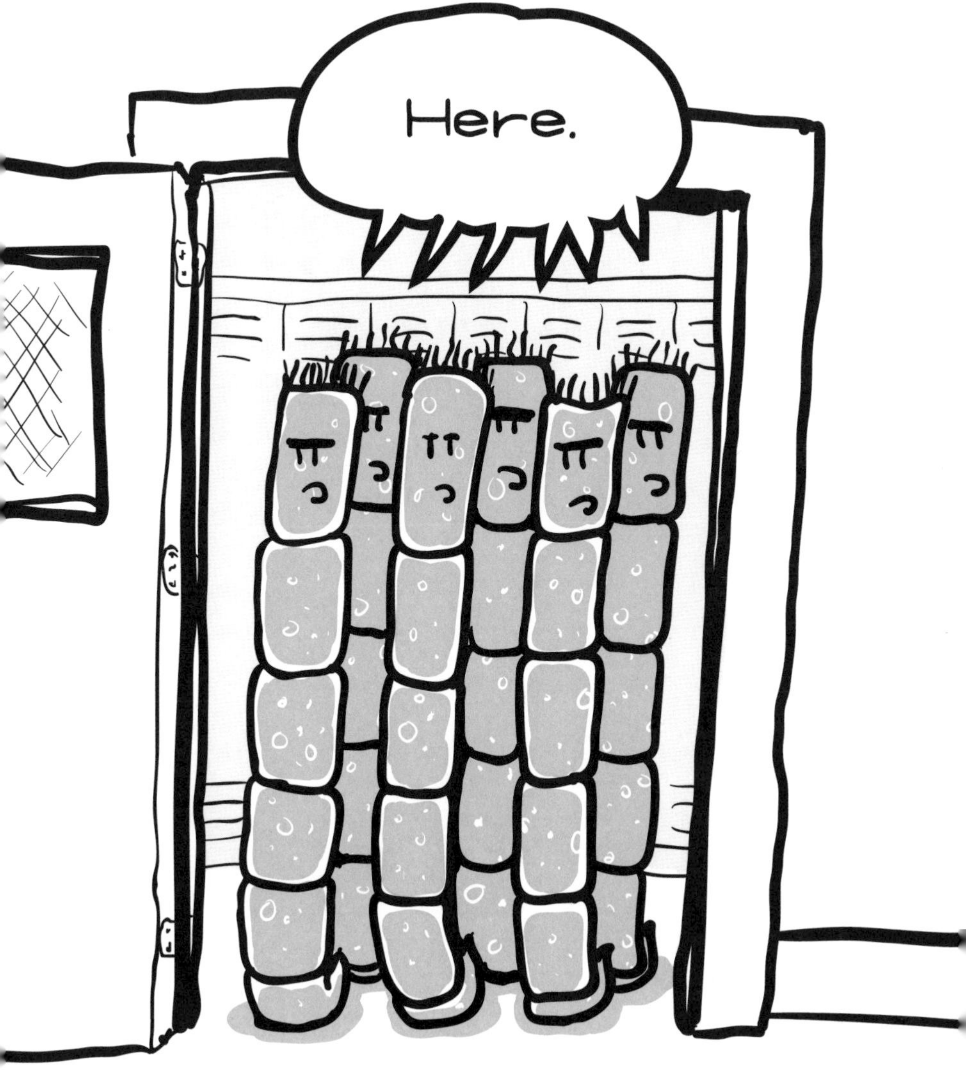

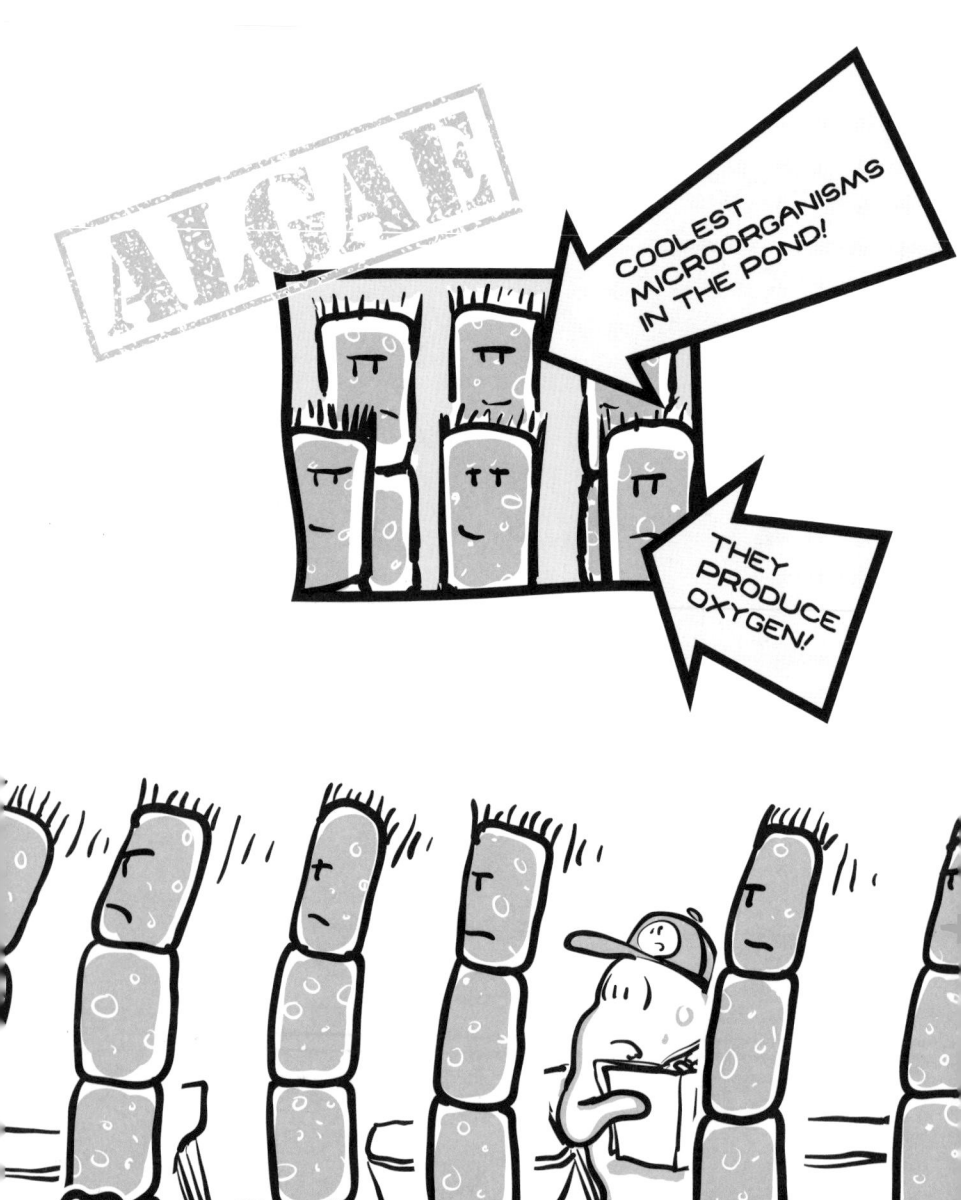

I know we are all going to have a great year here in the pond blah-blah-blah . . .

THE ADVENTURES OF SUPER AMOEBA!

SUPER AMOEBA?

ARE YOU THE PROTOZOANS?*
THE GREATEST CRIME-FIGHTING
TEAM OF ALL TIME?

THAT'S US.

WINK!

* PRO-TO-**ZO**-ANS**
** ONE-CELLED MICROSCOPIC ORGANISMS
THAT LIVE IN THE WATER***
*** WHEW! THAT'S ENOUGH SCIENCE FOR
ONE DAY!

WOW!
I LOVE YOU
GUYS!

WE'VE BEEN
HEARING A
LOT ABOUT
YOU.

ME?

GOOD
WORK.
ESPECIALLY
WITH
THAT
PLANT
MONSTER.

UH, THANKS!

WE WERE WONDERING IF YOU WANTED TO JOIN OUR CREW.

GASP! JOIN THE PROTOZOANS?

GET OUT OF THIS BACKWATER POND. COME TO THE BIG CITY.

WE'VE GOT A GREAT HEADQUARTERS.

AND A GREAT BENEFITS PACKAGE.

INCLUDING UNIFORMS.

- NO TRADING FOOD WITH ~~POD~~!
- ~~NO DETENTION!~~
- ~~DO NOT LET PEGGY EMBARRASS ME!~~
- GET PICKED FOR KICKBALL AT RECESS!
- SIT WITH COOL KIDS AT LUNCH!
- BE COOL!

Fresh start.

YOU'RE MAKING A LOT OF PROGRESS, DUDE! ONLY THREE TO GO AND YOU'RE OFFICIALLY THE SAME OLD SQUISH!

Uh, is anybody sitting here?

Panel 1:
You get delivery nachos?

Sure!

Panel 2:
Have a chip.

Panel 3:
Thanks!

Panel 4:
CRUNCH

MUNCH

Panel 5 (list):
- NO TRADING FOOD WITH POD!
- NO DETENTION!
- DO NOT LET PEGGY EMBARRASS ME!
- GET PICKED FOR KICKBALL AT RECESS!
- SIT WITH COOL KIDS AT LUNCH!
- BE COOL!

41

AFTER SCHOOL.

HE KIND OF LOOKS LIKE THAT BEANBAG CHAIR HE'S SITTING ON.

So, how was your first day of school, Squish?

SUPER AMOEBA!

HAVE THE COURAGE TO DO WHAT'S RIGHT!

NEW POND CITY LIMITS

45

THE HALL OF THE PROTOZOANS

FOR EMERGENCY USE ONLY

FOR EMERGENCY USE ONLY

FOR EMERGENCY USE ONLY

FOR EMERGENCY USE ONLY

FOR EMERGENCY USE

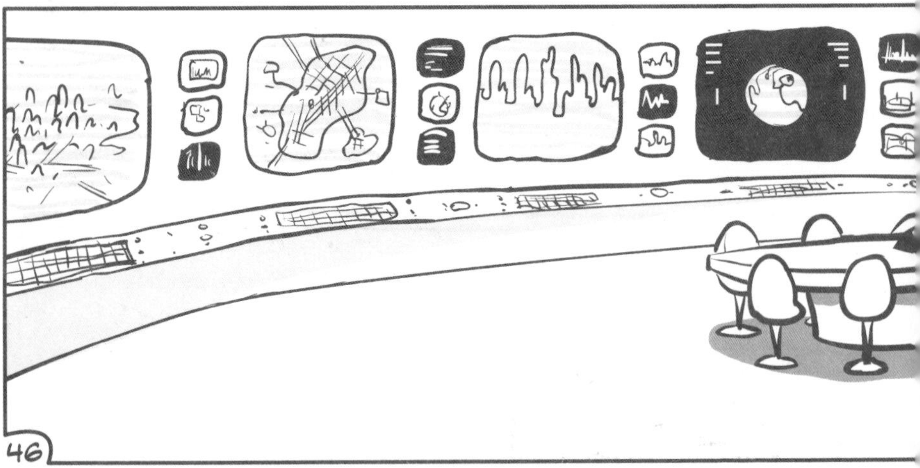

WOW.

THIS MAP SHOWS US WHEREVER THERE IS TROUBLE IN THE CITY.

COOL!

BZZT!
BZZT!

LOOKS LIKE THERE'S TROUBLE DOWNTOWN.

WHO'S COMING?

TAP TAP

CLICK!

BZZT!
BZZT!

50

TOSS!

Hmm...

We'll take the amoeba.

WOW!! SQUISH SURE IS SPENDING A LOT OF TIME WITH THE ALGAE LATELY!!!!

you mean, with the pond scum.

60

61

64

Hey, Squish.

Yeah?

See that amoeba over there? The **weird** one?

when the asteroid hits the pond, we're all gonna die. so then you won't need your lunch money.

He is a **little** weird, I guess.

When your nachos come tomorrow, don't eat them.

Huh?

- GET PICKED FOR KICKBALL AT RECESS!
- SIT WITH COOL KIDS AT LUNCH!
- BE COOL! ☆ ☆ ☆
- HUMILIATE YOUR FRIEND!
- BE CRUEL!
- KISS YOUR SOUL GOOD-BYE!

LOOKS LIKE YOUR LIST GOT LONGER.

Well?

... sure!

You asleep, Squish?

Yep!

SHOOP!

CLICK!

THE NEXT DAY.

NACHOS
TO YOUR DOOR

THE HALL OF THE PROTOZOANS

BACK AT THE HALL OF THE PROTOZOANS.

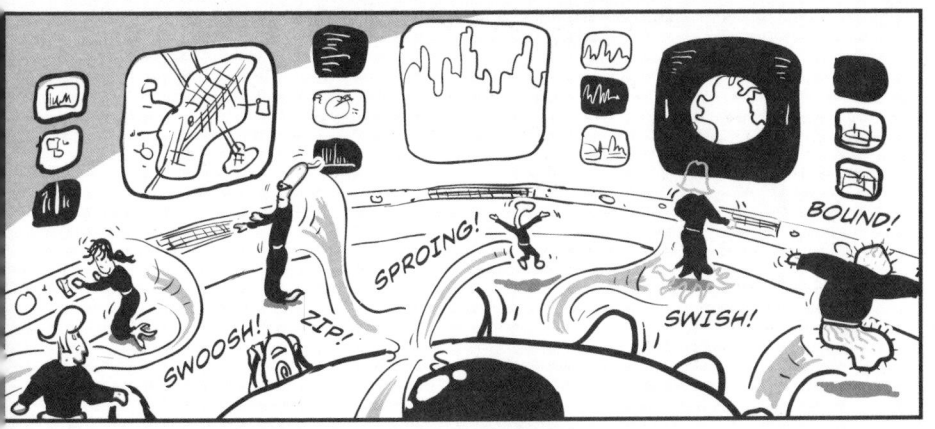

SWOOSH! ZIP! SPROING! SWISH! BOUND!

WE'LL SET UP A PERIMETER. SUPER AMOEBA, YOU'LL BE PART OF THE FIRST LINE OF DEFENSE.

NOD

ALERT: SMALL POND

BZZT! BZZT!

SMALL POND IS UNDER ATTACK!

IT'S JUST SMALL POND. *THE PROTOZOANS* HAVE BIGGER THINGS TO WORRY ABOUT.

RIGHT. BIGGER THINGS.

THANKS, SUPER AMOEBA!

Pod,
you can
always have
my nachos.

thanks.

Pfft. What did you expect from a little sack of jelly like that, anyway?

hey, squish—take two steps to the right.

SCOOT!

SCOOT!

OH NO! THE ALGAE JUST GOT WIPED OUT BY AN ASTEROID!! THAT'S SO SAD!!! GEE, I WONDER IF TOMORROW IS PIZZA DAY!

89

FUN SCIENCE WITH POD!

hey, kids. want to make slime?

it's easy. and fun.

get your supplies.

PLASTIC SANDWICH BAG

CORNSTARCH

WATER

GREEN FOOD DYE

YOU CAN DRAW THE ALGAE BROTHERS, TOO!! THEY ALL LOOK ALIKE!!!!!!

1.

2.

3.

4.

5.

6.

Give us your hat.

Sure!

IT'S GREEN...
IT'S BLOBBY...
IT'S GROSS...

IT'S squish!

DON'T MISS SQUISH'S NEXT *AMAZING, ACTION-PACKED ADVENTURE!*

COMING IN MAY 2012!

IF YOU LIKE *SQUISH*, YOU'LL LOVE *BABYMOUSE!*